Athens County
Library Services
Nelsonville, Ohio

D0776052

Books by Natalie Babbitt

Dick Foote and the Shark
Phoebe's Revolt
The Search for Delicious
Kneeknock Rise
The Something
Goody Hall
The Devil's Storybook
Tuck Everlasting
The Eyes of the Amaryllis
Herbert Rowbarge
The Devil's Other Storybook

The Devil's Other Storybook

The Devil's Other Storybook

Stories and Pictures by

NATALIE BABBITT

A Sunburst Book

Michael di Capua Books

Farrar · Straus · Giroux

*Athens County
Library Services
Nelsonville, Ohio*

Copyright © 1987 by Natalie Babbitt
All rights reserved
Library of Congress catalog card number: 86-32760
Published in Canada by Collins Publishers, Toronto
Printed in the United States of America
First edition, 1987
Sunburst edition, 1989

3 2000 00004 7556

CONTENTS

From his brimstone bed, at break of day,
    A-walking the Devil is gone,
To look at his little snug farm of the World,
    And see how his stock went on.

Over the hill and over the dale,
    And he went over the plain;
And backward and forward he swished his tail,
    As a gentleman swishes a cane.

ROBERT SOUTHEY (1774–1843)

The Devil's Other Storybook

THE FORTUNES OF
MADAME ORGANZA

THERE WAS a fortuneteller once who wasn't much good at her work. No matter who came to her door to get a fortune told, she could never think of any but the same old three: "You will meet a tall, dark stranger"; "You will take a long journey"; and "You will find a pot of gold." She went through the usual rigmarole, with a crystal ball and chanting, all in a gloomy little parlor lit with one candle, and she even wore a turban with a big glass jewel glued to it, right on the front where it showed. But of course, though this was very nice, the fortunes themselves were what mattered, and since none of them ever came true, it wasn't long before no one came to her door at all and she was forced to take in washing to keep herself going. But she kept the sign on her door saying FORTUNES BY MADAME ORGANZA—though her name in fact was Bessie—just in case.

Now, it happened that one dark night a couple of burglars eased through the village with a satchel of money stolen somewhere else, and they hid themselves in a barn, where in the morning they were discovered snoring away by the farmer; and he ran them off with a pitchfork so all-of-a-sudden that they had to leave the loot behind, buried in the haymow, and didn't dare go back.

Later the same morning, the farmer hired a milk-maid, who, being new to the place and no one thinking to warn her, went off with her first day's wages to get her fortune told. Madame Organza put on the turban, lit the candle, muttered and hummed for a while, and then said, "You will find a pot of gold."

"Goody!" said the milkmaid. And, tripping home, she climbed the ladder to the haymow to have a little peace and quiet for planning what she'd do when she was rich. And of course she sat down on the burglars'

satchel and pulled it out and opened it, and there was her gold, great handfuls of glittering coins, just as her fortune had predicted.

"Well! Goody again!" said the milkmaid. She closed up the satchel, climbed back down the ladder, and went to find the farmer. "Please," she said, "does this belong to you?"

"No," said the farmer, "it doesn't."

"Goody three!" said the milkmaid. "It's mine, then, and just what Madame Organza said I'd find." And she let the farmer peek inside at the gold. Then she went away to the city to begin a new life, and was never heard from again, though the farmer thought he saw her there, some time later, rolling by in a carriage, with plumes on her hat and a little white dog in her lap.

But in the meantime her story spread all over the village, and such a noise was made that down in Hell the Devil pricked up his ears and said, "What's that hullabaloo?" And when he found out what had happened, he smiled a big smile and straightaway went up to the World to see what he could do to cause a little extra trouble and confusion, for he'd guessed that

Madame Organza's business would be taking a turn for the better.

This was indeed the case. The line of people waiting to get their fortunes told stretched clear to the river and halfway back, with everyone so excited that everything else was forgotten. Cows were left unmilked, pigs unslopped, and bread sat so long in ovens that it burnt away to cinders. And Madame Organza, believing, herself, that she'd somehow got the knack of it at last, was telling fortunes at a great rate, though the fortunes were only the same old three from before.

During the days that followed, thanks to the Devil's interference, the village changed completely. Twenty-two people found pots of gold and went to live in the city, which they soon found dismal to the utmost but were too proud to say so. Another thirty-seven went off on long journeys, ending up in such spots as Borneo and Peru with no way at all to get back, and so they were forced, for a living, to chop bamboo or to keep herds of llamas in the Andes.

All the rest had met with tall, dark strangers who hung about, getting in the way, and looking altogether so alarming in their black hats and cloaks and their long black beards that the villagers remaining were afraid to stay and hurried to move in with relatives in other villages, which caused no end of bad feeling.

At last there was no one left but Madame Organza and the strangers, and since the strangers had the orphaned cows and pigs to care for and didn't want their fortunes told, Madame Organza put away her sign forever and went back full-time to being Bessie. She took in the strangers' washing, all of which was black, and made the best of it she could without complaining. And she put her crystal ball in the garden, where it showed to great advantage, out among the pansies, whenever the sun was shining.

JUSTICE

❧

THERE ARE few surprises in Hell. At least, the Devil has seldom been surprised—except for the time when someone spotted a rhinoceros.

"Absurd," said the Devil.

"I know it," said the major demon who'd brought in the news. "Nevertheless, I went and looked myself, and it's out there all right, large as life, with a hole right through its horn. It's out there shuffling and snuffling and breathing hard, and I'd say it looks impatient."

"I wonder what it wants," said the Devil. "Well, never mind. Perhaps it will go away."

Now, on this very day a man named Bangs arrived unexpectedly in Hell. Bangs was a mighty hunter who in life had crept about the wild parts of the World, shooting off his gun and making possible a steady stream of elephant's-foot umbrella stands and rabbit-fur muffs and reindeer-antler coatracks and other lovely, useful things, till on the day in question he backed by accident into a boa constrictor. And the boa constrictor, seizing both the opportunity and Bangs himself, constricted the hunter so hard that, before he knew it, he found himself at the gates of Hell, out of breath and very much surprised.

"This is a piece of luck!" said the Devil when Bangs was sent in to see him. "As it happens, you're the very type we need. We've got a rhinoceros loose, and we can't have it snorting about, upsetting people. Go out and catch it. Then we'll pen it up and charge admission."

"Well now," said Bangs, who'd recovered his breath and his swagger, "I don't put much store in bringing 'em back alive."

"Bangs, Bangs," said the Devil. "You've got a lot to learn. Guns are no earthly use down here. You'll have to do the job with a net. But be careful. This rhinoceros has a hole right through its horn and I'm told it looks impatient."

"A hole right through its horn?" said Bangs, turning pale.

"That's the situation," said the Devil.

"Dear me," said Bangs. "I may be the one who made that hole."

"I wouldn't be a bit surprised," said the Devil. "Now, run along and do what you're told."

So Bangs had to take a big rope net and creep out into the wild parts of Hell to look for the rhinoceros, and it goes without saying that, without his gun, he was very much afraid he would find it. He looked all the rest of the day and never saw a thing, but he could hear the shuffling and the snuffling and the breathing hard, always just out of sight. At sundown, however, he was setting up his tent when out through the bushes burst the rhinoceros, like a bus downhill with no brakes, and it chased Bangs all night long, up and down the wild parts till daybreak. And then it disappeared.

This happened three times in a row, and at last Bangs dragged in to see the Devil. "Look here," he said. "I'm supposed to be chasing that rhinoceros, I know, but instead, somehow, it's chasing me. It chases me all night long, and then it disappears. I can't go on like this— I'll be worn to a frazzle."

"Go on?" said the Devil. "Of course you'll go on. You'll catch it sooner or later. I'm depending on you, and I don't want to see you again till the job is done."

So Bangs dragged back to the wild parts. He tried to sleep in the daytime, but this was hard to do, what with the shuffling and the snuffling and the breathing hard always just out of sight. And as soon as the sun went down in the evening, the rhinoceros would burst through the bushes and chase him up and down till morning.

After three weeks of this, Bangs was worn to a frazzle, and so were his boots. He gave up the chase altogether and took to living as wild animals do, always watchful, always listening, sleeping with one eye open. And he dug himself a hole to hide in. But as sure as he came out at night to cook his supper, there was the rhinoceros, and off they would go, pounding through the wild parts till the sun came up at dawn.

"Well," said the Devil after a while, "I guess Bangs is doing the next best thing. He may not be catching that rhinoceros, but at least he's keeping it busy."

"True enough," said the major demon.

"Might as well leave him to it, then," said the Devil. "Pass the word that the danger's taken care of."

So the major demon passed the word and everyone felt relieved. And every month or so the Devil sent someone out with fresh hay for the rhinoceros and a new pair of boots for Bangs—just to keep things even.

THE SOLDIER

THERE WAS a soldier once who had nothing at all to do because, though he'd often been to war, at this particular time there wasn't one to fight in, anywhere around. So he did what he could—he kept his sword shiny, and polished his boots, and he practiced marching on an open road, up and down, up and down, with his plumes and tassels bouncing and the buttons on his jacket flashing in the sun, and the sight of him was altogether splendid.

One day the Devil came along, disguised as an old, old man with a weak knee and a strong crutch, and he stopped when he saw the soldier. "I say!" exclaimed the Devil. "What an elegant picture you make!"

The soldier gave him a smart salute. "Thank you, old man," he said. "I'm practicing my marching."

"So I see," said the Devil. "But why aren't you off somewhere, fighting?"

"There's no war anywhere to fight in, dash it," said the soldier, with a sigh.

"Don't despair," said the Devil. "Something will turn up soon."

"I hope so," said the soldier, "for there's nothing I like even half so much. I've seen some lovely wars, old man, some lovely wars."

"Ah!" said the Devil. "I don't for a moment doubt it."

"I fought against the Turks at Heliopolis," said the soldier proudly.

"Yes?" said the Devil. "I was there."

"Well—but I also fought in the Santo Domingo Rebellion," said the soldier.

"I was there," said the Devil.

"Indeed!" said the soldier, with a frown. "However, *I* was with Napoleon at Austerlitz."

"I was there," said the Devil.

"Hmm," said the soldier. "You've seen a few campaigns yourself."

"Oh, yes," said the Devil. "In fact, I never miss one."

"Then," said the soldier, "I suppose you'll say you were there at Waterloo."

"I was there," said the Devil.

The soldier raised one eyebrow. "Come, come, old man," he said. "Next you'll be telling me you fought in the Siege of Troy and went with Caesar into Gaul!"

"That's right," said the Devil. "I was there."

The soldier tried to hide a smile, for he didn't at all believe what he was hearing. But, deciding to be polite, he said, "It seems I've got a ways to go to match you."

"Yes," said the Devil, "you do."

"Well," said the soldier, smiling once again behind his sleeve, "I must be getting on with my marching. Perhaps we'll meet again at the next great battle."

"Perhaps we will," said the Devil, "for I'll certainly be there." And he moved off down the road, leaning on his crutch, and didn't try at all to hide his own smile.

BOATING

❀

SOME PEOPLE think Hell is dry as crackers, but
this is not the case. There are four nice rivers inside
the walls, and a fifth, called the Styx, that flows clear
round the place outside.

Hell has the Styx the way castles have moats, but
there isn't any drawbridge. Instead, you have to come
across the water on a ferryboat run by a very old man
named Charon. Most of the time Charon does his job
all by himself, but it happened one day that he came
to the throne room with a problem.

"What's wrong?" said the Devil, putting aside the
novel he was reading.

"Why," said Charon, "they're having some kind of

fuss in the World, in case you didn't know it."

"They're always having fusses in the World," said the Devil with a yawn. "What of it?"

"Well, whatever sort of fuss it is," said Charon, "they're coming down in droves and I can't keep up. You'll have to lay on another ferryboat."

"You don't say!" said the Devil. "That's splendid! I'll come and take a look."

And sure enough, there were hordes of people on the far side of the Styx, waiting to get across. Some of them were quite put out to be kept there cooling their heels, and wouldn't stay nicely in line for a minute. And what with their birdcages, boxes, and bags all piled and getting mixed, the confusion was indescribable.

"I'm doing the best I can," said Charon to the Devil, "but you see the way things are."

"Hmmm," said the Devil. "Well now. I'll give you a hand myself. It looks like fun."

He called for a second ferry—which was, like Charon's, more of a raft than a boat—and, climbing aboard, seized the pole and pushed out cross-current into the river Styx. He wasn't as good at it as Charon, not having had the practice, but still arrived not too long after at the opposite bank, where all the people were waiting.

"Ahoy," said the Devil. "Women and children first." And since there weren't any children—indeed, there never are—three old women stepped onto the raft, which was all there was room for, and off they started back across the river.

"And who, my dears, may you be?" asked the Devil, eyeing their silks and feathers.

"We're sisters," said the first old woman. "The last of an important old family. The sort of people who matter."

"We can't imagine what we're doing here with all these common types," said the second.

"It's all a terrible mistake," said the third.

"Indeed!" said the Devil, with a smile. "I'll have someone look into it."

"I should hope so," said the first old woman. "Why, we can't put up with this! Look at these dreadful people you've got coming in—riffraff of the lowest sort! It would appear that anyone at all can get in."

"We can't be expected," said the second, "to mingle with peasants and boors."

"Never in the World," said the third.

"It's true," said the Devil, "that we do have every class down here. But so, I've heard, does Heaven."

"I don't believe it," said the first old woman. "Not Heaven."

"You must be misinformed," said the second. "Only the best people go to Heaven."

"Otherwise," said the third, "whyever call it Heaven?"

"An interesting point," said the Devil. "Why, indeed!"

And all the way across the river Styx the three went on protesting and explaining.

When the raft at last scraped up before the gates, the sisters refused to get off. "We simply can't go in," said the first old woman. "I'm sure you understand."

"Oh, I do," said the Devil. "I do."

"Not our grade of people in the least," said the second.

"Look into it for us, won't you?" said the third.

"We'll just wait here and catch the next boat back."

Now, the river Styx flows round the walls of Hell in a wandering clockwise direction, and a long way round it is, too, which will come as no surprise. And though the current isn't swift, it's steady. So the Devil, disembarking, put his pole against the ferry and simply shoved it out again so that the current bore it off, turning it gently in circles, with the sisters still on board. And then he went back to his throne room and sent a minor demon out to give a hand to Charon. For the Devil had had enough and wanted to finish his novel.

Years went by, and dozens of years, with the sisters still floating round the walls of Hell. Every once in a while, in the beginning, the Devil would remember them and go out when it was time for them to pass. And as they came along, he could hear their protestations, steady as the current of the Styx.

"Ragtag and bobtail," they'd be saying. "Waifs and strays. Quite beneath contempt! Commoners, upstarts, people of the street. Not our sort at all." And they would say, "There's been some mix-up, certainly. Why don't they get it straightened out?"

Sometimes they saw the Devil standing on the banks, and the first old woman would call to him, "Yoo-hoo! I say, my good man—have you made inquiries concerning our situation?" And the Devil would wave and nod, and watch as they slowly circled by and disappeared. And then he would smile and go back through the gates for a nice cold glass of cider. But after a time he forgot the three completely. This was not because he was too busy to remember. No, indeed. He forgot them because they weren't the sort of people who matter.

HOW AKBAR WENT TO
BETHLEHEM

☙

THERE ARE no camels in Hell. You might suppose there would be, for camels have shocking bad tempers; they were crabby to begin with, when everything was new, and they're just as crabby now. The only thing a camel does from morning to night is sulk and moan about in the desert, kicking its children—who always kick back—and complaining in a voice that is not at all agreeable. But still, there are no camels in Hell. Not anymore.

Once, long ago, when Hell was getting settled, there *was* a camel there, a great, ragged beast named Akbar, and the place was just to his liking. He was the Devil's special pet, and could go where he pleased, growling and grumbling and curling his long, split lip at everyone. "Oh, Akbar," the Devil would say, "what a satisfaction you are!" And Akbar would sneer and show his yellow teeth, the picture of disrespect, and the Devil would laugh and let him get away with it. So it seemed like a nice arrangement.

Then one night when it was winter in the World, a strange light appeared in the sky that had never been there before. Everyone in Hell observed it, and they all crowded into the throne room—major and minor demons, and imps of various ages—to find out what it meant.

The Devil had seen it, too, and was very much upset, though of course he didn't let on. "It's only a star," he said. "You've all seen stars before."

"But not like this one," said the demons. "Never one like this. We don't know what to make of it!" And one of the youngest imps began to cry.

"It's nothing, I tell you," said the Devil snappishly. "Go along to bed and leave me be."

But when they had gone, he climbed to the roof of his throne room and stared at the strange new light in the sky above the World, for he knew very well what had happened. A baby had been born up there who was going to be nothing but trouble for a long, long time to come. "Confound it," said the Devil to himself. "And just when I was getting on so well!"

Now, although this event was a terrible thing for the Devil, he still felt a certain curiosity. So, one dark night soon after, he dressed himself as an Arab, climbed onto Akbar's hump, and away they went up to the World to see how things were going. They wandered up and down among the little towns and found them all so quiet and serene that the Devil felt encouraged. "No fuss here," he thought. "It all seems just the same." But he didn't dare go to the one small town where the strange light glowed the brightest.

It happened, however, that soon they arrived at a wild and dry sort of place with cold black sand, and wind that made the Devil shiver, huddled on Akbar's hump. And, wandering there to think things over, the Devil saw at last three beasts, not far away, striding by on the crest of a rounded dune. Camels they were, like Akbar, but hung with bells and tassels and richly patterned rugs. They held their heads high as they came, and on their backs, on saddles made of skins and polished wood, were riders in robes of pale, soft wool woven into stripes and fine designs, with wide, embroidered borders traced in gold. Gold was on their fingers, too, and round their necks, and one wore a thin gold crown. Their faces were lit by the glow that hung low now in the sky, and they were leaning toward it, eager and intent.

"Look at that," said the Devil to Akbar. "They're going *there*, to see that baby, or I miss my guess." And he tried to look scornful, but the sight made him very uneasy.

However, instead of sneering with him, Akbar made a sound in his curving throat, a gentle sort of bleat. And then, quite suddenly, he dropped to the big, knobbed knees of his two front legs, pitching the Devil off onto the sand.

"What's this?" cried the Devil. "How dare you!"

But Akbar continued to kneel, with his ragged head tipped down, till the royal camels disappeared from sight. And then he reared upright again, and this time

made a great, glad, bubbling sound like a trumpet full
of milk, and strode away alone in the wake of the
wonderful three, off toward the strange new glow.

"Confound it!" yelled the Devil. "*You* can't go!"

But Akbar could. And did. And the Devil was afraid
to go after him.

Next morning, down in Hell, everyone said,
"Where's Akbar?"

And the Devil said, "Who cares? We don't want *his*
sort here."

And never again did he try to keep a camel.

THE SIGNPOST

THERE WAS a pair of sweethearts once named Gil and Flora who believed they were in love. But, in fact, they were not a bit good for each other. They were always quarreling over nothing, and would go for days quite red in the face, refusing to speak to each other. Then they would make it up, and things would be fine until the next argument. At last they had the worst argument of all, and Gil said to Flora, "I've had enough. I'm going away to the inn at Argo and I'll wait there seven days. If you can promise you'll never argue again, send me a message and I'll come back and marry you."

And Flora said, "You can go to the inn at Argo and

stay there forever, for all I care. Because it's you that argues, not me."

So Gil went off quite red in the face and started on foot down the road.

Now, the road went along for many miles and then it divided in two, going east to Argo and west to a town called Woolfield. There was a signpost at the split, with arrows pointing the way to each. And when Gil arrived at the signpost, he headed east and came in time to Argo, where he went to the inn to wait.

Four days went by, and at home Flora stewed and fretted and missed Gil more and more. Finally she could stand it no longer. She wrote a note to him saying, "Come back right away and marry me, and I'll try never ever to argue." And she hired a messenger with a fast horse who went galloping toward Argo with the note tucked into his vest.

But on that very day the Devil was walking about in the World, looking for ways to make mischief, and came by chance to the place where the road divided. "Well!" said the Devil. "Here's a nice idea." He switched the signpost around so that the arrow for Argo pointed now to Woolfield, and the arrow for Woolfield pointed instead to Argo. And then he went on his way, whistling a little tune, and so far as anyone knows never passed that way again, at least not for years and years.

Meanwhile, Flora's messenger came galloping along and, arriving at the signpost, turned west, thinking he was heading for Argo. And of course, after a while, he arrived in Woolfield instead and went to Woolfield's inn to look for Gil. But though he searched it from top to bottom, he could find no trace; so he sat himself down to have a mug of ale and catch his breath before he turned back to Flora with the news that Gil was gone.

While this was going on, Gil stewed and fretted at the Argo inn and said to himself, "Four days! And I miss her more and more. I'll just go and marry her, arguments or no." So he left the inn and hurried back along the road, coming at last to the signpost. "Egad!" he said. (In those days people often said *Egad*.) "Egad, what's this? I haven't been in Argo at all but in Woolfield. And it could be that Flora has sent a message already and I wasn't there to get it!" Off he went at a run toward Woolfield, thinking he was headed right, this time, for Argo. And on the way he might have passed the messenger coming from the other direction, but the messenger had ridden his horse into a meadow to drink at a little stream, so they missed each other entirely.

Gil arrived at the Woolfield inn, and he waited out the last three days. But no message came. "Well, that's it, then," he said. "She doesn't want me back. I'll go away to the city and seek my fortune." So that is what he did.

And the messenger, arriving home, told Flora that Gil had been nowhere to be found. "Well," said Flora, "that's it, then. He doesn't want me back. I'll have to marry someone else." So that is what *she* did.

And a peddler who knew both Argo and Woolfield came along soon after and set the signpost straight.

Gil found his fortune in the city and married a lovely girl named Belle with whom it never occurred to him to argue. And Flora married a lovely man named Carl with whom she lived in peace without a single quarrel. And down in Hell, the Devil, who'd long since forgotten the signpost, heard of these two happy couples and said to himself, "Disgusting. How do such things happen?"

LESSONS

THERE WAS a sharp-eyed parrot once who lived
with a doting old woman and was her pride and joy.
His name was Columbine, and instead of growing up
with pirates, and learning all kinds of nasty language,
he had spent his youth with a clergyman and acquired,
in his earliest lessons, another kind of language altogether. Then, having outlived the clergyman—for
parrots survive to amazing great ages—he moved to
the old woman's cottage, where he learned to say things
like "Sweetheart, kiss me quick," and was just as well
content. Still, Columbine was no sissy. He was big and
shrewd and liked things on the up-and-up. And to keep
them that way, he sat all day on his perch in the old

woman's window, with his eye peeled, and he watched for trouble.

The old woman's cottage was on the main road, and all day long the carts went by, and the wagons, and people on horseback or muleback or clumping along on foot, going from here to there and Heaven knows where else. And Columbine looked hard at everyone. When someone went by who looked suspicious, he'd say "*Oh*-oh," or "Look out," or sometimes even "Lock the doors!" But there wasn't any need for locks with Columbine around. He was better than any lock or bolt, or even any watchdog, just by the way he sat in the window with his eye peeled.

Now, one day it happened that the Devil came down the road disguised as a strolling musician with a fiddle under his arm. Columbine saw through the costume in a minute—that's how sharp his eye was—and he squawked, "It's the Devil! The Devil! Fire! Flood! Pestilence! Run for your lives!" And while he was squawking, he flapped his wings something awful, and hopped up and down, and made such a racket that the old woman hid under the bed.

The Devil stopped in the middle of the road, right in front of the cottage. "Shh!" he hissed to Columbine. "Hush up, you wretched bird—you'll give the game away!" But Columbine wouldn't hush up; he went on flapping, with his feathers every which way, squawking out his warnings at the top of his lungs. And of course the people in the road went running off in great alarm and confusion. Horses reared, carts were overturned, and even the mules were in a hurry. And soon there was no one left except the Devil, alone and feeling foolish, with the fiddle under his arm.

"Drat," said the Devil. "That ties it. There's not a soul in sight."

Columbine calmed down. He closed one eye and said, "Pretty bird."

"You there," said the Devil. "Suppose I were to trample your beak in the dust?"

"Bibles," said Columbine, very cool and clear.

The Devil backed off a step. "What?" he said, surprised.

"Church," said Columbine. "Church and chapel. And cathedral."

The Devil backed off even farther.

"Parson," said Columbine. "And priest. Parson, pastor, priest, and preacher. And *Pope*."

"Whoo!" said the Devil with a shiver. And he took himself off in a cloud of smoke and went back down to Hell.

The road soon filled up again with traffic, and the old woman came out from under the bed and went on baking bread. And Columbine sat on his perch and preened his feathers, but he kept his eye peeled just the same, for he was not so pleased with himself that he thought of neglecting his duty.

Down in Hell, the Devil trampled the fiddle in the dust and said to himself, "Someone ought to teach that bird a lesson." But, of course, someone already had, thank goodness.

THE FALL AND RISE
OF BATHBONE

❧

THERE WAS a little, sweet no one of a man once, named Bathbone, who was not quite right in the head, for he thought he was someone else—a famous opera singer of the time called Doremi Faso. No one was sure how Bathbone had got this notion. He had never sung a note in his life, though he hummed sometimes, and on top of that, there was the fact that he was little and sweet, whereas the real Doremi Faso was quite the opposite, with the shape and weight of a walrus and the ego of several roosters. Still, here was Bathbone, sure they were one and the same.

Faso, though famous, was not a very good singer. His

voice was big and deep, but big and deep like a moose at the bottom of a well. He was only famous because someone important had once *said* he was a good singer, right out in the newspapers, printed in type and everything, and after that nobody had the nerve to say he wasn't. But Bathbone didn't know this. He was only sure that he was Faso and that Faso was he, and no amount of talk could change his mind.

Things went along this way for quite a while, and then one night Faso met his end at the opera when he gave himself a stroke on a high note he had no business trying for, and he turned up in Hell at once, ego and all, to begin a long series of concerts. Meanwhile, his death was reported in the newspapers. Bathbone, reading of it, was very much astonished. "What can this mean?" he said. "Here I am, the great Doremi Faso, as hale and hearty as ever. How can they say I am dead?" He took to puzzling back and forth on a bridge across a river, waving his arms and mumbling, while he tried to figure it out. And it wasn't long before he waved and mumbled himself right off the edge and into the water, where he drowned. But the newspapers ignored this second loss and ran, instead, a story about someone who'd grown a four-foot-long mustache.

Now, when Bathbone fell off the bridge, there was a hasty conference in Heaven. And it was decided that Bathbone had better go to Hell and get himself straight as to who he really was. For in Heaven they like you to know that kind of thing and be content with it. So Bathbone arrived at the gates of Hell, still mumbling and wet from head to foot, and was sent to see the Devil.

"What's this?" said the Devil.

"It is I," said Bathbone, "the great Doremi Faso."

"Oh, no, it isn't," said the Devil. "We've got one of those already. I know about you. You're Bathbone, that's who, and you're dripping all over my carpet."

"Sir," said Bathbone, drawing himself up as tall as he could, "I am not Bathbone. My name is Doremi Faso and my death was reported in the newspapers."

The Devil looked annoyed. "Bathbone," he said, "you're not quite right in the head. Now, listen. You don't belong down here, and we don't want you. You're much too little and sweet. But I've been informed you have to stay till you get at the truth on this business of who you are. So I'll tell you one more time: you're not Doremi Faso. The real Doremi Faso has been down here for a week. He's giving a concert right this very minute."

"I don't believe it," said Bathbone.

"Then come and see for yourself," said the Devil.

So off they went to the concert hall. And there on the stage was the real Doremi Faso, bellowing out some song or other, and striking remarkable poses. But the rows and rows of seats were empty—not a single soul to listen—and no one to play in the orchestra, either. All the instruments lay silent, though on some of Faso's high notes a cello, leaning in a corner, shuddered its strings faintly.

"See?" said the Devil.

But Bathbone said, "That can't be Faso. That man up there is a terrible singer. And, for another thing, there's nobody here to listen. Why, people come in droves to hear the great Faso sing."

"Not down here they don't," said the Devil with satisfaction. "Down here, no one ever comes."

"Just my point, if you'll excuse me," said Bathbone. "The singer on that stage is an impostor."

"You're a stubborn man, Bathbone," said the Devil. "Well, all right. We'll schedule a concert for you. Tomorrow, after you've got dried out. And then we'll see who's who."

The next afternoon, the concert hall was full, and roared with the sound of laughter and talk, while up and down the aisles, hawkers were selling peanuts and beer. In the orchestra pit, the musicians were tuning their instruments with a dreadful discord of tweets, blats, and scrapings. The racket was immense, and in the midst of it all, the orchestra conductor came up to Bathbone, who was waiting in the wings, and said, "So—what are you planning to sing?"

And Bathbone said, " 'Out of My Soul's Deep Longing.' "

The conductor made a face. "The Devil won't like that one very much," he said, "but if it's what you want, we'll do it." He went away and, appearing below in the orchestra pit, lifted his baton. The chandeliers went dim, the shadowy great hall fell silent. And Bathbone, full of confidence, stepped out onto the stage. Down came the baton, up rose the music, with the flutes and violins fighting for the melody. And Bathbone began to sing:

> *Out of my soul's deep longing,*
> *These little songs come winging*
> *Like wee feather'd birds . . .*

He had never sung a note before. His voice came out little and sweet, not big and deep like Faso's, and took him so much by surprise that by the time he'd got to "wee feather'd birds" he simply stopped, unable to manage one more note, and the truth swelled up in his heart like a great balloon and exploded, leaving him shocked and limp. "Why, they're right," he exclaimed to himself. "I'm not the great Doremi Faso!"

The people in the audience stood up, jeering and throwing peanuts, and when they got tired of that, they all filed out and went about their business. Even the musicians and the orchestra conductor wandered off, leaving Bathbone quite alone in the middle of the stage, feeling very sad. "I guess," he said aloud, "I'm only Bathbone after all."

As soon as the words were out of his mouth, a blaze

of light leapt up, and Bathbone vanished, simply disappeared, and was never ever seen in Hell again. And when the Devil was told, he said, "Good. That's done, then."

Bathbone is singing now in a glee club in Heaven with his own name—B A T H B O N E—on the posters, and the people come in droves to hear him. He is famous there for the songs that require in their solos a little, sweet voice, and the flutes and violins are something wonderful.

Oh, and by the way, the real Doremi Faso still sings every day in Hell, and has got an audience at last—a walrus and several roosters. They go through an awful lot of peanuts, but they seem to enjoy the music.

SIMPLE
SENTENCES

❦

ONE AFTERNOON in Hell, the Devil was napping in his throne room when a frightful hubbub in the hall outside brought him upright on the instant. "Now what?" he barked. "Can't I get a minute's peace?"

The door to the throne room opened and a minor demon stuck his head in. "Sorry," said the minor demon, "but we've got two new arrivals here and they're giving me fits with their entry forms."

"Show them in," said the Devil darkly. "I'll straighten them out."

So the minor demon brought in the two and stood them before the Devil, where the first one, a shabby, mean-looking rascal, dropped his jaw and said, "Well, I'll be sugared! If it ain't Old Scratch hisself!"

And the second, a long-nosed gentleman, opened his eyes wide and said, "Dear me—it's Lucifer!"

Now, the Devil isn't fond of fancy names like Lucifer, preferring simply to be called "the Devil" or, once in a while, "your Highness." And he certainly dislikes all disrespectful terms, of which Old Scratch is only one. So he scowled at the two who stood there, and said, "See here—I like things peaceful in Hell. We can't have all this rattle and disruption."

At which the two said, both at once, "But—"

"Hold on for half a second, can't you?" said the Devil testily. He turned to the minor demon. "What've you got on the pair of them so far?" he demanded.

The minor demon consulted the sheaf of papers he'd brought in with him. "This one," he said, pointing with his pencil to the rascal, "is in for picking pockets. And that one"—pointing to the long-nosed gentleman—"is down for the sin of pride and for writing books no one could understand."

"Well?" said the Devil. "That sounds all right. What's the matter with that?"

"But it's not a question of their sins," said the minor demon. "We've known about those for years. What it is is what happened up there that finished them off, don't you know. And I can't get their stories straight on that."

"Oh," said the Devil. "All right." And he turned to the two, who'd been waiting there, glaring at each other. "You," he said to the rascal. "What's *your* story?"

"All I know is," said the rascal in a whiny voice, "I was mindin' my own business, out on the public streets, when this lardy-dardy lamps me and commences screechin' fit to blast yer ears. Thinks I, 'This cove is off his chump,' so I do a bunk. But he shags me, and we both come a cropper in the gutter and sap our noodles, and—well—that pins the basket. Next thing I know, I'm standin' here ramfeezled and over at the knees, and he's comin' the ugly like I'm the party responsible."

"What?" said the Devil.

"If I may be permitted," sniffed the long-nosed gentleman. "What actually transpired is that this squalid and depraved illiterate was on the verge of appropriating my purse when I observed the action at the penultimate moment. And whilst I was attempting to apprehend him, we both seem to have stumbled on a curbstone, with resultant fractures and contusions, and I find I've been deprived of my life—and my hat—in a most abrupt and inconvenient fashion. Surely I can't be censured for reacting with extreme exasperation."

"What?" said the Devil.

"I think what they mean is—" began the minor demon.

"I know what they mean," said the Devil. "That one tried to pick this one's pocket. Just write it down like that."

"Chalk your pull, there," cried the rascal. "You've got it in the wrong box. Maybe I was on the filch, sure, that's my job. But I wasn't after this poor, mucked-out barebones, not for toffee. I know his type. More squeak than wool, you can stand on me for that. A barber's cat like him ain't never got a chinker to his name. Why, I'd go home by beggar's bush if I couldn't pick better than that!"

"What?" said the Devil.

"He means—" the minor demon tried again.

"I know what he means," said the Devil. "He means he *didn't* try to pick the other one's pocket. A misunderstanding. So just write it down like that."

"Oh, now, really," exclaimed the long-nosed gentleman. "I must protest. I tell you, I saw this felon's grubby hand reaching for my purse. I am not in the habit of misinterpreting evidence supplied by my own observations. Why, the meanest intelligence could easily discern that the fellow's a thoroughgoing prevaricator!"

"See what I mean?" said the minor demon to the Devil.

"I see," said the Devil.

The rascal stepped a little nearer to the Devil. "Look here, yer honor," he said. "I don't want to tread the shoe awry and chance yer gettin' magged. But it's above my bend how a chap with yer quick parts could hang in the hedge when it comes to separate between brass tacks and flimflam. I mean, this underdone swellhead could argue the leg off an iron pot, but it's still all flytrap. Take it from me."

The long-nosed gentleman stepped forward then, himself. "I'm cognizant of the fact," he said haughtily, "that I'm not by any stretch of the imagination in Paradise. And it may be that I'm naive to expect impartiality. All I can do is to iterate the unembellished fact that I observed what I observed, and what I observed was that this clumsy brigand tried to rob me."

The rascal narrowed his eyes. "Handsomely over the bricks there, puggy," he said in a threatening tone. "Clumsy, am I? Just because you've got yer head full of bees, that's no reason to draw the longbow. You never twigged me doin' *my* kind of work. Even if I was on the dip with a piker like you, you wouldn't twig me. When it comes to light fingers, I'm the top mahatma. No one ever twigs me. So play Tom Tell-Truth or else keep sloom."

The long-nosed gentleman's face turned very red. "Sir," he said in a strangled voice, "your impertinence is beyond all sufferance. I wouldn't dignify your statements with rebuttals if it weren't that I have such respect for veracity. And the plain, unvarnished truth is, you attempted to commit a felony."

The Devil clapped his hands with a sound like a pistol going off. "That's enough," he said. "I've heard enough. The plain, unvarnished truth is there's only one crime here: neither of you can speak a simple sentence."

And at this they both stopped short to gape at him, and both said, *"What?"*

The Devil turned to the minor demon. "Write down," he said, "that what happened was they both tripped over their tongues."

The minor demon nodded. "Very well. And what shall I put for their punishment?"

For the first time, the Devil smiled. "We'll put them in together, in a room designed for one," he said. "And there they'll stay till it all freezes over down here."

So the two were led away, both sputtering with shock, and the minor demon folded up his papers. "I do admire that punishment," he said to the Devil.

"Thank you," said the Devil, settling back to get on with his nap. "It was the simplest sentence I could think of."

THE EAR

THERE WAS a clan of very silly people called the Pishpash once, ages and ages ago, who took it into their heads to carve a huge stone idol at the top of a hill, and when it was finished, they sat and sang it songs with words like *zum zum zum*, and they gave it offerings of turnips, which grew wild in the area around. The idol had the head of a hairless man with ears as big as washtubs, and its body was shaped like a horse sitting down, and needless to say, it didn't care a bit about turnips—or anything else, for that matter. So the turnips went bad, lying there in heaps, and they smelled something awful. Nevertheless, the Pishpash kept right on piling new turnips on top of the old, and believed something good would come of it. Nothing did, however, and at last a minor earthquake tipped the idol over. Its body was broken to bits, and the head cracked off and rolled like a boulder down the hill, coming to rest with one ear up, one ear down, out on a level plain below. The Pishpash were put off by this, and took it for an evil omen, so they packed up their bowls and spears and babies and wandered off, no one is sure exactly where, but it doesn't matter because, although the Devil found them entertaining, they were all of them very silly, and good riddance to the lot. The head, however, remained behind and lay there so long that the earth began to cover it up, until finally, after hundreds of years and a lot more minor earthquakes, it was buried under three or four feet of soil.

By that time, things were civilized. A village had appeared, and a great many little farms, and everyone mostly raised turnips, since they grew so well there. And one day some new people came to the place and picked out a spot for farming that was near where the idol's head lay resting underground. These people were a father and a mother and their big, slow son,

Beevis. They put up a shack to live in, and next they tried to figure out where to dig a well.

"It ought to be over there," said Beevis.

"No, here," said Mother, "next to the shack."

"Not here," said Father. "Too risky. Beevis would only fall into it."

"Would not," said Beevis.

"Probably would, at that," said Mother.

"Would *not*," said Beevis, who had got his feelings hurt. "You never listen to me." And this was true. They didn't.

In any case, the end of it was that Beevis was sent to dig the well exactly at the spot where the idol's head was buried. The digging took a while because Beevis was big but he wasn't very strong, and with his feelings hurt he wasn't inclined to hurry. "They never listen to me," he said, this time to himself, as he chunked away at the soil with his shovel. Still, slow as he was, after a little while he had dug down to the place where his shovel went *chink* instead of *chunk*. "Rock," said Beevis. He brushed away the soil at the bottom of the hole to see how large the rock might be, and there, exposed to the sunlight after all those years and earthquakes, was the Pishpash idol's ear, big as a washtub but plainly an ear for all that, and altogether unexpected.

Beevis climbed out of the hole and stood gazing at the ear for a long, long time, so long that at last his father came over and stood beside him.

"Why aren't you digging, Beevis?" said Father.

"There's an ear down there," said Beevis.

"What?" said Father.

"An ear," said Beevis, pointing. "Down there."

So Father looked and saw the ear as plain as day at the bottom of the hole. And then they both stood gazing at it.

After a while, Mother peered through a window of the shack and called, "What in the World are you doing?"

Father beckoned to her, so out she came and looked down into the hole. "What's that?" she said.

"It's an ear," said Father. "Beevis found it."

"It's ugly," said Mother.

"Button your lip," said Beevis. "It'll hear you."

And indeed, at that very moment, a minor earth-

quake shook the ground just hard enough to make their feet tingle.

"It heard you," said Beevis.

After this, they went inside the shack to talk it over.

"It's a dangerous ear, that's clear enough," said Mother. "If it can make the ground shake."

"Likely so," said Father. "What do you think we should do?"

"I think," said Mother, "we should cover it up. Fill in the hole again."

"No!" said Beevis. "That ear is mine. I found it, and I like it."

"Cover it up, Beevis," said Father. "It's the only thing to do. Go out right now and fill in the hole."

"You never hear a word I say," said Beevis. He went back out to the hole and stood there, looking down at the ear. *"Zum zum zum,"* he crooned softly so that no one but the ear could hear him.

"Fill in the hole, Beevis," called Father from the shack, so Beevis picked up his shovel and pretended to begin. But when they weren't watching, he took some boards left over from the shack and laid them across the top of the hole and covered them over with dirt so that it looked as if he'd done what they told him. And then he went and dug the well in quite another spot, on the opposite side of the shack.

The weeks went by with no more earthquakes. Beevis and Mother and Father plowed their field and planted turnips and nothing more was said about the ear. But every night, when the old folks were asleep, Beevis would creep out and uncover the ear and talk to it. He told it all his troubles, and he tried out all his thoughts about life and the World, and the ear, lit up by moonlight shining into the hole, would listen to every word. And every night he would croon to it ever so softly— *zum zum zum*—before he covered it up again. But he never gave it turnips, for Beevis wasn't silly like the Pishpash.

These midnight meetings with the ear did a lot for Beevis. He began to feel more confident. He stood up straighter, and wasn't nearly so slow.

"Beevis has changed since we came here," said Father to Mother. "He's turning into quite a man!"

"Fresh air, hard work, and healthy food," said

Mother, who was cooking up turnips at the stove. "That, and no mollycoddling. That's what's done it."

So of course it was clear they didn't understand at all.

And then one night, while Beevis was out in the moonlight, talking to the ear and explaining his dreams for the future, Mother woke up and went to the window and saw him. "Beevis!" she called. "What in the World are you doing?"

"Phooey," said Beevis to the ear. "Looks like the jig is up."

But not at all. No sooner were the words out of his mouth than a more-than-minor earthquake shook the land so hard you'd have thought the whole place was a dust mop. The shack fell down, and so did Mother, and out on the other side, the walls of the well collapsed. And Father got a bump on the knee when the stove fell over. But Beevis, standing by the ear, wasn't so much as toppled off his feet, and the walls of the ear's hole stayed firm.

Next day, when they'd calmed themselves down, Mother said, "It's an evil omen. We'd better leave this place. It's no good after all."

And Father said, "Beevis, pack up what's still in one piece and we'll move along."

"I'll pack," said Beevis, "but I won't leave. I like it here."

For once, they heard him. "But, Beevis," said Mother, "how will you manage without us?"

"I'll manage," said Beevis. "I'll manage very well. It's time."

And it was. Beevis managed. He waved goodbye to Mother and Father and sent them on their way. He rebuilt the shack and dug a new well. Then he pulled up all the turnips and planted beets instead, and became a successful farmer. And he made a round sort of cover for the ear's hole and told people it was a dry well and to keep away, which they did, having no reason not to. And every night, unless it rained, Beevis went out in the moonlight and told his hopes and joys to the ear. And every night the ear heard every word.

J   ATHENS   c.2

Babbitt Babbitt, Natalie.
         The Devil's
     other storybook :
     stories and
     pictures

WITHDRAWN

J